The Berenstain Bears
and the
GHOST OF THE FOREST

Off go the Bear Scouts
to camp out all night.
Will an unwelcome ghost
visit their site?

A FIRST TIME READER™

The Berenstain Bears
and the
GHOST OF THE FOREST

Stan & Jan Berenstain

Random House 🏠 New York

Copyright © 1988 by Berenstains, Inc. All rights reserved under International and Pan-American Copyright Conventions. Published in the United States by Random House, Inc., New York, and simultaneously in Canada by Random House of Canada Limited, Toronto.

Library of Congress Cataloging-in-Publication Data:
Berenstain, Stan. The Berenstain bears and the ghost of the forest. (A first time reader) SUMMARY: Papa Bear's attempt to scare a band of young campers by telling them about ghosts in the woods comes to an unexpected conclusion with a double ghost lesson. [1. Ghosts—Fiction. 2. Camping—Fiction. 3. Bears —Fiction. 4. Stories in rhyme] I. Berenstain, Jan. II. Title. III. Series: Berenstain, Stan. First time reader. PZ8.3.B4493Bfr 1988 [E] 88-42586 ISBN: 0-394-80565-8 (pbk.); 0-394-90565-2 (lib. bdg.)

Manufactured in the United States of America 1 2 3 4 5 6 7 8 9 0

"Look out for Papa,"
said Brother Bear
as the Bear Scouts
tiptoed down the stair.

"We won't need Pa,"
Sister Bear said.
"Not this trip,"
agreed Cousin Fred.

"I see you Scouts
are on your way
into Great Spooky Forest
for an overnight stay!"

"Pa! I hope you'll excuse us,"
said Brother Bear.
"But this is a trip
we'd rather not share."

"It's also a trip
I'd rather not share.
Me sleep with spooks?
Not on a dare!"

"Spooks?" gasped the Scouts,
not a little afraid.

"Spooks of all kinds!
A nightly parade!

"And boss of them all—
the Ghost of the Wood!
Call off the trip, Scouts.
I really and truly
think you should!"

"Nonsense!" said Mama,
who overheard.
"Spooks, indeed!
Not another word!

"Your papa's just trying
to give you a scare.
So, be off with you, Scouts,"
smiled wise Mama Bear.

As the Scouts waved good-bye
to Mama Bear,
Pa sneaked around
and climbed the stair.

Then up to the attic
to the old-rag box.
What's Papa up to,
the sly old fox?

Sly Papa cut
three holes in a sheet
and turned himself into
a ghost with bear feet.

Leader Jane met the Scouts
at the edge of the wood.
"No Papa?" she asked.
"That's very good."

"Papa gave us
a bit of a fright.
He said there are spooks
and they come out at night!"

"Spooks? That's nonsense! Now let me explain— THERE ARE NO SUCH THINGS!" said Scout Leader Jane.

So the Scouts went to work
setting up camp—
raising the tent,

filling the lamp,

building the fire,
getting it lit.

Jane took time
to explore a bit.

She collected some leaves.
She studied some seeds.
That's when she heard
a voice in the weeds.

Chuckling and talking
to himself in there
was—you guessed it—
Papa Q. Bear!

"This trick will be fun,"
Papa Bear said
as he pulled the sheet
over his head.

"Hmm," said Jane
as she tiptoed away.
"This is a game
that two can play!"

Then using twigs
and leaves as a base,
she started to make
what looked like...

A FACE!

The Scouts told stories
in the firelight.
Then they all
bedded down for the night.

They heard it just
as they started to doze.
It frightened those Scouts
from their heads to their toes.

They ran to Jane's tent.
But Jane wasn't there.
"W-what shall we do?"
cried Sister Bear.

Then, a spookier spook
came into sight,
and gave the *first* ghost
a terrible fright.

WHO-O-O-O

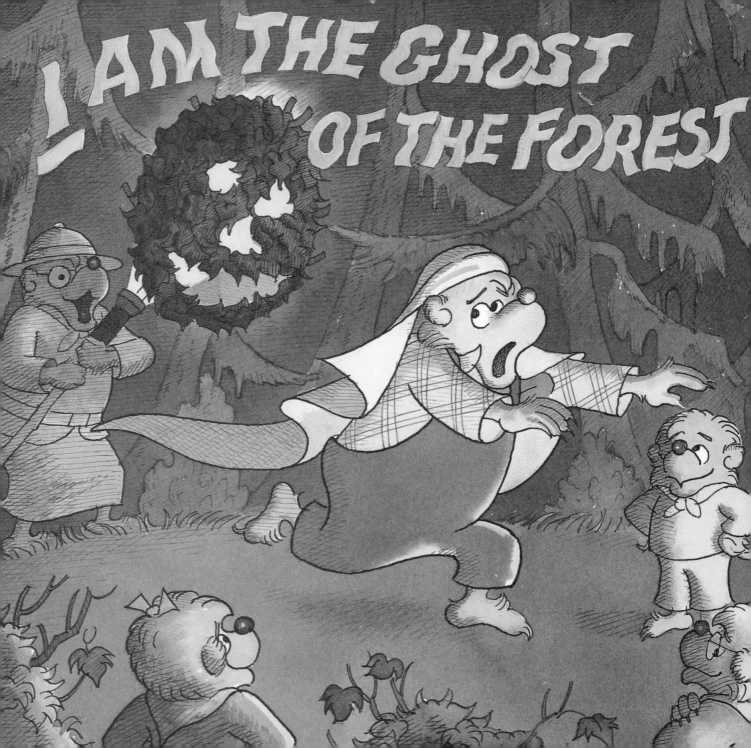

And who did Spook Two
turn out to be?
Leader Jane, of course.
That's when they saw—
SPOOK NUMBER THREE!

As the campers and Pa
shivered and shook,
Sis opened an eye
and took a good look.
She saw something strange:
a yellow hat on a pumpkin head,
Pa's red pajamas
and a polka-dot dress
that looked exactly like...MAMA'S!

"Just having fun!"
The voice—it was Mama's.
Then her head poked out
of Papa's pajamas.

"Teaching Papa
a lesson like this
was just too good
a chance to miss!"

"It's a double ghost lesson,"
said Jane with a grin.
"There are no such things!
There never have been!

"But just as sure
as night follows day—
it's fun to be scared
of them anyway!"